Daniel O'Connell

The Irish Patriot: Daniel O'Connel's Legacy to Irish Americans

Daniel O'Connell

The Irish Patriot: Daniel O'Connel's Legacy to Irish Americans

ISBN/EAN: 9783337303105

Printed in Europe, USA, Canada, Australia, Japan

Cover: Foto ©Andreas Hilbeck / pixelio.de

More available books at **www.hansebooks.com**

THE

IRISH PATRIOT.

DANIEL O'CONNEL'S LEGACY TO IRISH AMERICANS.

PHILADELPHIA:
PRINTED FOR GRATUITOUS DISTRIBUTION.

ADDRESS FROM THE PEOPLE OF IRELAND

TO THEIR COUNTRYMEN AND COUNTRYWOMEN IN AMERICA.

DEAR FRIENDS: You are at a great distance from your native land! A wide expanse of water separates you from the beloved country of your birth—from us and from the kindred whom you love, and who love you, and pray for your happiness and prosperity in the land of your adoption.

We regard America with feelings of admiration: we do not look upon her as a strange land, nor upon her people as aliens from our affections. The power of steam has brought us nearer together; it will increase the intercourse between us, so that the character of the Irish people and of the American people must in future be acted upon by the feelings and dispositions of each.

The object of this address is to call your attention to the subject of slavery in America—that foul blot upon the noble institution and the fair fame of your adopted country. But for this one stain, America would indeed be a land worthy your adoption; but she will never be the glorious country that her free Constitution designed her to be, so long as her soil is polluted by the foot-prints of a single slave.

Slavery is the most tremendous invasion of the natural, inalienable rights of man, and of some of the noblest gifts of God, "life, liberty, and the pursuit of happiness." What a spectacle does America present to the people of the earth! A land of professing Christian republicans, uniting their energies for the oppression and degradation of three millions of innocent human beings, the children of one common Father, who suffer the most grievous wrongs and the utmost degradation, for no crime of their ancestors or their own! Slavery is a sin against God and man. All who are not for it must be against it. None can be neutral. We entreat you to take the part of justice, religion, and liberty.

It is in vain that American citizens attempt to conceal their own and their country's degradation under this withering curse. America is cursed by slavery! WE CALL UPON YOU TO UNITE

WITH THE ABOLITIONISTS, and never to cease your efforts until perfect liberty be granted to every one of her inhabitants, the black man as well as the white man. We are all children of the same gracious God; all equally entitled to life, liberty, and the pursuit of happiness.

We are told that you possess great power, both moral and political, in America. We entreat you to exercise that power and that influence for the sake of humanity.

You will not witness the horrors of slavery in all the States of America. Thirteen of them are free, and thirteen are slave States. But in all, the pro-slavery feeling, though rapidly decreasing, is still strong. Do not unite with it: on the contrary, oppose it by all the peaceful means in your power. JOIN WITH THE ABOLITIONISTS EVERY WHERE. They are the only consistent advocates of liberty. Tell every man that you do not understand liberty for the white man, and slavery for the black man; that you are for liberty for all, of every color, creed, and country.

The American citizen proudly points to the National Declaration of Independence, which declares that all mankind are born free and equal, and are alike entitled to life, liberty, and the pursuit of happiness. Aid him to carry out this noble declaration, by obtaining freedom for the slave.

Irishmen and Irishwomen! treat the colored people as your equals, as brethren. By all your memories of Ireland, continue to love liberty—hate slavery—CLING BY THE ABOLITIONISTS—and in America you will do honor to the name of Ireland.

[Signed by]   DANIEL O'CONNELL,
THEOBALD MATHEW.

And *sixty thousand* other inhabitants of Ireland.

LETTER FROM JAMES HAUGHTON, ESQ.

TO IRISHMEN IN AMERICA:

COUNTRYMEN:—My heart often prompts me to address you in a few words of kindly remonstrance. I wish you so to conduct yourselves in the distant land you have made your home, as that your conduct may reflect honor on the loved country you have left behind you, and cause you to be really respected by the people among whom you now dwell. These advantages can be secured only by a steady adherence, on your part, to the principles of truth and honor, which you should make the guiding star of your life.

You love liberty for yourselves. Be consistent in your advocacy of this universal right of the human race; and claim it as the inalienable privilege of all men,—of the colored man, as well as the white man.

I fear too many of you have forgotten your duty, in this respect, and that thus the fame of Ireland—which we should shield from the breath of dishonor—is sullied in the eyes of those who should only see reflected in your conduct, evidence of the firm determination of your countrymen to stand fast by the noble principles of Christian rectitude.

In the twelfth century, the synod of Armagh proclaimed liberty to every captive in Ireland, and since then, a slave has never polluted our green isle.

Remember the faithfulness of O'Connell. Let his memory, which is embalmed in many of our hearts, and his whole life, which was a consistent course in favor of civil and religious liberty, be a beacon-light guiding you in your career. Demand, as he did, that freedom for all which you claim as your own birthright.

Thus, and thus alone, can you secure true respect for yourselves, and cause the stranger to say of your country, "If I were not an American, I should be proud to be an Irishman."

By all your pleasant memories of Ireland; by her glorious mountains and her beautiful valleys; by her verdant plains, which are watered by the streams in which you loved to disport yourselves in childhood; by your love of these things; by your affection for your kindred and friends, and by your reverence for almighty God,—I appeal to you, and I ask you to love your fellow-men of all complexions and of all creeds, and to demand for them all, the exact measure of justice you claim for yourselves.

The sad moan of four millions of slaves comes across the broad ocean, and it sounds painfully in our ears. I ask you to aid in turning their sorrow into joy—to aid in enabling the fathers and mothers of the colored race in America to clasp their little ones, and feel all the happiness and all the responsibility of being their guardians and their guides, from infancy up to manhood. Turn not a deaf ear to the cry of the slave, but let him feel, in future and for evermore, that in every Irishman he has a friend.

Whatever may be your rank or condition in the land of your adoption, believe me, countrymen, you can only acquire and maintain an honorable reputation there, by such a course of conduct as I recommend; and whatever may be your practice, whether in consonance with, or in opposition to these sentiments, I feel assured that you will say in your hearts, "He is right." I entreat you to act manfully in accordance with your convictions, and I beg to subscribe myself,

Faithfully yours,

JAMES HAUGHTON.

DUBLIN, 35 Eccles Street.

SLAVERY NOT A DEBATABLE QUESTION.

An American gentleman waited upon me this morning, and I asked him, with some anxiety, "What part of America do you come from?" "I came from Boston." "Do me the honor to shake hands. You came from a State that has never been tarnished with slavery—a State to which our ancestors fled from the tyranny of England, and the worst of all tyrannies, the odious attempt to interfere between a man and his God; a tyranny that I have in principle helped to put down in this country, and wish to put down in every country upon the face of the globe. (Cheers.) It is odious and insolent to interfere between a man and his God; to fetter with law the choice which the conscience makes of its mode of adoring the eternal and adorable God. I cannot talk of toleration, because it supposes that a boon has been given to a human being, in allowing him to have his conscience free: (Cheers.) It was in that struggle," I said, "that your fathers left England, and I rejoice to see an American from Boston; but I should be sorry to be contaminated by the touch of a man from those States where slavery is continued." (Cheers.) "Oh," said he, "you are alluding to slavery: though I am no advocate for it, yet if you will allow me, I will discuss that question with you." I replied, that if a man should propose to me a discussion on the propriety of picking pockets, I would turn him out of my study, for fear he should carry his theory into practice. (Laughter and cheers.) "And, meaning you no sort of offence," I added, "which I cannot mean to a gentleman who does me the honor to pay me a civil visit, I would as soon discuss the one question with you as the other." The one is a paltry theft:

"Who steals my purse, steals trash; 'tis something, nothing;
'Twas mine, 'tis his, and has been slave to thousands"—

but he who thinks he can vindicate the possession of one human being by another—the sale of soul and body—the separation of father and mother—the taking of the mother from the infant at her breast, and selling the one to one master and the other to another—is a man whom I will not answer with words—nor yet with blows, for the time for the latter has not yet come. (Cheers.)—DANIEL O'CONNELL.

EXTRACTS FROM THE SPEECHES OF O'CONNELL.

I now come to America, the boasted land of freedom; and here I find slavery, which they not only tolerate but extend, justified and defended as a legacy left them by us. It is but too true. But I would say unto them, you threw off the allegiance you owed us, because you thought we were oppressing you with the Stamp Act. You boasted of your deliverance from slavery. On what principle, then, do you now continue your fellow-men in bondage, and render that bondage even more galling by ringing in the ears of the sufferers from your tyranny, what you have done, what you have suffered, for freedom? They may retaliate upon us. They may reply by allusions to the slaveries we have established or encouraged. But what would be thought of that man who should attempt to justify the crime of sheep-stealing, by alleging that another stole sheep too? Would such a defence be listened to? Oh, no; and I will say unto you, freemen of America, and the press will convey it to you almost as swift as the wind, that God understands you; that you are hypocrites, tyrants, and unjust men; that you are degraded and dishonored; and I say unto you, dare not to stand up boasting of your freedom or your privileges, while you continue to treat men, redeemed by the same blood, as the mere creatures of your will; for while you do so, there is a blot on your escutcheon which all the waters of the Atlantic cannot wash out.

*　　*　　*　　*　　*　　*　　*

Of all men living, an American citizen, who is the owner of slaves, is the most despicable; he is a political hypocrite of the very worst description. The friends of humanity and liberty, in Europe, should join in one universal cry of shame on the American slaveholders? "Base wretches," should we shout in chorus—"base wretches, how dare you profane the temple of national freedom, the sacred fane of republican rites, with the presence and the sufferings of human beings in chains and slavery?"—*Speech delivered at an Anti-Slavery Meeting in 1829.*

I speak of liberty in commendation. Patriotism is a virtue, but it can be selfish. Give me the great and immortal Bolivar, the saviour and regenerator of his country. He found her a province, and he has made her a nation. His first act was to give freedom to the slaves upon his own estate. (Hear, hear.) In Colombia, all castes and all colors are free and unshackled. But how I like to contrast him with the far-famed northern heroes! George Washington! that great and enlightened character,—the soldier and the statesman,—had but one blot upon his character. He had slaves, and he gave them liberty when he wanted them no longer. (Loud cheers.) Let America, in the fullness of her pride, wave on high her banner of freedom and its blazing stars. I point to her, and say, There is one foul blot upon it; you have negro slavery. They may compare their struggles for freedom to Marathon and Leuctra, and point to the rifleman with his gun, amidst her woods and forests, shouting for liberty and America. In the midst of their laughter and their pride, I point them to the negro children screaming for the mother from whose bosom they have been torn. America, it is a foul stain upon your character! (Cheers.) This conduct, kept up by men who had themselves to struggle for freedom, is doubly unjust. Let them hoist the flag of liberty, with the whip and rack on one side, and the star of freedom upon the other. The Americans are a sensitive people; in fifty-four years they have increased their population from three millions to twenty millions; they have many glories that surround them, but their beams are partly shorn, for they have slaves. (Cheers.) Their hearts do not beat so strong for liberty as mine. * * * * I will call for justice, in the name of the living God, and I shall find an echo in the breast of every human being. (Cheers.)—*Speech delivered at the Annual Meeting of the Cork Anti-Slavery Society, 1829.*

Ireland and Irishmen should be foremost in seeking to effect the emancipation of mankind. (Cheers.) * * * * * * The Americans alleged that they had not perpetrated the crime, but inherited it from England. This, however, fact as it was, was still a paltry apology for America, who asserting liberty for herself, still used the brand and the lash against others. (Hear.) He taunted America with the continuance of slavery; and the voice with which he there uttered the taunt would be wafted on the wings of the press, until it would be heard in the remote wilds of America; it would be wafted over the waters of the Missouri and those of the Mississippi; and even the slaves upon the distant banks of the Ohio would make his words resound in the ears of their heartless masters, and tell them to their face, that they were the victims of cruelty, injustice, and foul oppression. (Cheers.) Bright as was the page of American history, and brilliant as was the emblazonment of her deeds, still, negro slavery was a black, a "damning spot" upon it. Glorious and splendid as was the star-spangled banner of republican America, still it was stained with the deep, foul blot of human blood.—*Speech delivered at a Meeting of the Dublin Anti-Slavery Society*, 1830.

Man cannot have property in man. Slavery is a nuisance, to be put down, not to be compromised with; and to be assailed without cessation and without mercy by every blow that can be leveled at the monster. * * * * * Let general principles be asserted. And as it is the cause of religion and liberty, all that is wanted is the unwearied repetition of zealous advocacy to make it certainly triumphant. Let every man, then, in whatever position he may be placed, do his duty in crushing that hideous tyranny, which rends the husband from the wife, the children from their parents; which enables one human being, at his uncontrolled will, to apply the lash to the back of his fellow-man.—*Speech delivered at the London Anti-Slavery Society*, 1830.

We are responsible for what we do, and also for the influence of our example. Think you that the United States of America would be able to hold up their heads among the nations,—the United States, who shook off their allegiance to their sovereign, and declared that it was the right of every man to enjoy freedom—of every man, whether black, white, or red; who made this declaration before the God of armies, and then, when they had succeeded in their enterprise, forgot their vow, and made slaves, and used the lash and the chain,—would they dare to take their place among the nations, if it were not that England countenances them in the practice?—*Speech delivered at the General Meeting of the British Anti-Slavery Society*, 1831.

My claim to be heard on this occasion is included in one sentence— I am an Abolitionist. (Cheering.) I am for speedy, immediate abolition. (Renewed cheers.) I care not what caste, creed, or color, slavery may assume. Whether it be personal or political, mental or corporeal, intellectual or spiritual, I am for its total, its instant abolition. (Great applause.) I enter into no compromise with slavery. I am for justice, in the name of humanity, and according to the law of the living God.

*   *   *   *   *   *

The time has now come, when every man who has honest feelings should declare himself the advocate of abolition. He who consents to tolerate crime is a criminal; and never will I lose the slightest opportunity, whether here or in the legislature, or any where else, to raise my voice for liberty,—for the extinction of slavery. (Great applause.) Humanity, justice and religion combine to call upon us to abolish this foul blot. But it is not England or Britain alone that is stained with this crime. The democratic Republic of America shares in the guilt. Oh! the inconsistency of these apostles of liberty talking of freedom, while they basely and wickedly continue the slavery of their fellow-men, the negroes of Africa! A republican is naturally proud and high-minded, and we may make the pride of the North American republicans the very weapon by which to break down slavery; for, if the example of England were gone, they could not, in the face of the world, continue the odious and atrocious system one moment longer. (Cheers.) Abolish it throughout the British colonies, and away it goes in America. (Renewed cheers.)

* * * * * * *

Slavery is a crime, a high crime against Heaven, and its annihilation ought not to be postponed. We have lately heard a good deal of the iniquity of the East India Company, getting money from the poor, infatuated wretches who throw themselves beneath the wheel of Juggernaut's car. This is lamentable indeed; but what care I, whether the instrument of torture be a wheel or a lash? (Applause.) I am against Juggernaut, both in the East Indies and West Indies, and am determined, therefore, not to assist in perpetuating slavery. Is it possible, that where humanity, benevolence and religion are combined, there can be doubt of success? The priests of Juggernaut are respectable persons compared with those who oppose such a combination, (applause); and I entreat you to assist in the great work by becoming its apostles.—*Speech delivered before the London Anti-Slavery Society, 1831.*

I will now go to America. I have often longed to go there, in reality; but so long as it is tarnished by slavery, I will never pollute my foot by treading on its shores. (Cheers.) In the course of my Parliamentary duty, a few days ago, I had to arraign the conduct of the despot of the North, for his cruelty to the men, women and children, of Poland; and I spoke of him with the execration he merits. But, I confess, that although I hate him with as much hatred as one Christian man can hate another human being, viz.: I detest his actions with abhorrence, unutterable and indescribable; yet there is a climax in my hatred. I would adopt the language of the poet, but reverse the imagery, and say,

"In the deepest hell, there is a depth still more profound,"

and that is to be found in the conduct of the American slave-owners. (Cheers). They are the basest of the base—the most execrable of the execrable. I thank God, that upon the wings of the press, the voice of so humble an individual as myself will pass against the western breeze—that it will reach the rivers, the lakes, the mountains, and the glens of America—and that the friends of liberty there will sympathize with me, and rejoice that I here tear down the image of Liberty from the recreant hand of America, and condemn her as the vilest of hypocrites—the greatest of liars. (Long continued cheers.)

When this country most unjustly and tyrannically oppressed its colonies, and insisted that a Parliament of borough-mongers in Westminster should have the power of putting their long fingers across the Atlantic into the pockets of the Americans, taking out as much as they pleased, and, if they found anything, leaving what residuum they chose—America turned round, and appealed to justice, and she was right; appealed to humanity, and she was right; appealed to her own brave sword, and she was right, and I glory in it. At that awful period, when America was exciting all the nations of the world; when she was declaring her independence, and her inhabitants pledged their lives, their fortunes, and their sacred honor, and invoked the God of charity (whom they foolishly called the God of battles, which he is not, any more than he is the God of murder)—at that awful period, when they laid the foundation of their liberty, they began with these words: " We hold these truths to be self-evident; that all men are created equal; that they are endowed by their Creator with certain inalienable rights; that among these are life, liberty, and the pursuit of happiness." Thus the American has acknowledged what he cannot deny, viz., that God the Creator has endowed man with those inalienable rights. But it is not the white man, it is not the copper-colored man, nor is it the black man alone, who is thus endowed; it is all men who are possessed of these inalienable rights. The man, however, who cannot vote in any State assembly without admitting this as the foundation of his liberty, has the atrocious injustice, the murderous injustice, to trample upon these inalienable rights; as it were, to attempt to rob the Creator of his gifts, and to appropriate to himself his brother man, as if he could be his slave. (Cheers.) Shame be upon America! eternal shame be upon her escutcheon! (Loud cheers.)

Shortly there will not be a slave in the British colonies. Five lines in an Act of Parliament, the other night, liberated nearly 500,000 slaves in the East Indies, at a single blow. The West Indians will be obliged to grant emancipation, in spite of the paltry attempts to prevent it; and we will then turn to America, and to every part of Europe, and require emancipation. (Cheers.) No! they must not think that they can boast of their republican institutions—that they can talk of their strength and their glory. Unless they abolish slavery, they must write themselves down liars, or call a general convention of the States, and blot out the first sentence of their Declaration of Independence, and write in its place, "Liberty in America means the power to flog slaves, and to work them for nothing." (Loud applause.) * * * *

The voice of Europe will proclaim the slave's deliverance, and will say to him, "Shed no blood, but take care that your blood be not shed." I tell the American slave-owner, that he shall not have silence; for, humble as I am, and feeble as my voice may be, yet deafening the sound of the westerly wave, and riding against the blast as thunder goes, it shall reach America, telling the black man that the time for his emancipation has come, and the oppressor that the period of his injustice is soon to terminate! (Cheers.)—*Speech delivered at the Great Anti-Colonization Meeting in London,* 1833.

Mr. O'Connell presented himself to the meeting, amid the most enthusiastic cheers. After some remarks of a general nature, the Hon. and learned gentleman proceeded to speak in terms of severe censure of the conduct of the Americans, in continuing to keep in bondage the black population in many of their States. He did not wonder at the death plagues of New Orleans, or the devastation of its people, many of whom enjoyed health and vigor at morn, and were lifeless at noon, when they had committed or countenanced crimes which could only be registered with the annals of Nicholas and the curses of Poland.

The Hon. and learned gentleman read several extracts from an American slaveholding Act, in which it was enjoined that no judge, legislative member, barrister or preacher, should speak or write anything against slavery, under the pain of being sentenced to not less than three years, and not more than twenty-one years' imprisonment, or death, at the discretion of the court!!! And that no American should teach a

11

slave to read or write, under the pain of not less than three months, and not more than twelve months' imprisonment. (Hear, hear.) The Hon. and learned gentleman flung this black dishonor on the star-spangled banner of America—in vain did it wave over every sea, proclaiming the honor of the boasted republic of modern times—those who fought under it were felons to the human race, (hear, hear,) traitors to liberty, to their own honor, and blasphemers of the Almighty. "The red arm of God," continued the Hon. and learned gentleman, "is bared; and let the enemies of those whom his Son died to save, the black man as well as the white man, beware of its vengeance! The lightning careers through the troubled air resistless, amidst the howling of the tempest and rolling of the thunder. Oh, for one moment of poetic inspiration, that my words, with the fire of indignation with which my bosom burns, may be borne on the western breeze across the wide Atlantic, light on their shores, reverberate among their mountains, and be wafted down the rivers of America!"—*Speech delivered at an Anti-Slavery Meeting in London*, 1835.

He had given the Americans some severe but merited reproofs; for which they had paid him wages in abuse and scurrility. He was satisfied that they had done so. He was accustomed to receive such wages in return for his labors. He had never done good but he was vilified for his pains; and he felt that he could not sleep soundly were such opponents to cease abusing him. (Cheers.) He would continue to earn such wages. (Cheers.) By the blessing of God, he would yet trample on the serpent of slave-owning cupidity, and triumph over the hiss of the foul reptile, which marked its agony, and excited his contempt. The Americans, in their conduct toward their slaves, were traitors to the cause of human liberty, and foul detractors of the democratic principle, which he had cherished throughout his political life, and blasphemers of that great and sacred name which they pretended to reverence. In reprobation of their disgraceful conduct, his public voice had been heard across the wide Atlantic. Like the thunder-storm in its strength, it had careered against the breeze, armed with the lightning of Christian truth. (Great cheering.) And, let them seek to repress it as they may; let them murder and assassinate in the true spirit of lynch law; the storm would wax louder and louder around them, till the claims of justice became too strong to be withstood, and the black man would stand up, too big for his chains. It seemed, indeed—he hoped what he was about to say was not profanation—as if the curse of the Almighty had already overtaken them. For the first time in their political history, disgraceful tumult and anarchy had been witnessed in their cities. Blood had been shed without the sanction of law, and even Sir Robert Peel had been enabled—but ho was here in danger of becoming political. (Cries of No, no—Go on, and cheers.) Well, then, even Sir Robert Peel had been enabled to taunt the Americans with gross inconsistency and lawless proceedings. He differed from Sir Robert Peel on many points. (Laughter.) Every body knew that. (Renewed laughter.) It was no doubt presumption in him to differ from so great a man, but yet such was the fact. (Laughter.) On one point, however, he fully agreed with him. Let the proud Americans learn, that all parties in this country unite in condemnation of their conduct; and let them also learn that the worst of all aristocracies is that which prevails in America—an aristocracy which had been aptly denominated that of the human skin. The most insufferable pride was that shown by such an aristocracy. And yet he must confess that he could not understand such pride. He could understand the pride of noble descent. He could understand why a man should plume himself on the success of his ancestors in plundering the people some centuries ago. He could understand the pride arising from immense landed possessions. He could even understand the pride of wealth, the fruit of honest and careful industry. Yet when he thought of the color of the skin making men aristocratic, he felt his astonishment to vie with his contempt. Many a white skin covered a black heart; yet an aristocrat of the skin was the proudest of the proud. Republicans were proverbially proud, and therefore he delighted to taunt the Americans with the superlative meanness, as well as injustice, of their assumed airs of superiority over their black fellow-citizens. (Cheers.) He would continue to hurl his taunts across the Atlantic. And, oh!—but perhaps it was his pride that dictated the hope—that some black O'Connell might rise among his fellow slaves, (tremendous cheers,) who would cry, Agitate, agitate, (renewed cheering,) till the two millions and a half of his fellow-sufferers learned the secret of their strength—learned that they were two millions and a half. (Enthusiastic cheers.) If there was one thing which more than another could excite his hatred, it was the laws which the Americans had framed to prevent the instruction of their slaves. To be seen in company with a negro who could write, was visited with imprisonment, (shame!) and to teach a slave the principles of freedom was punished with death. Were these human laws, it might be asked? Were they not laws made by the wolves of the forest?—No—they were made by a congregation of two-legged wolves—American wolves—monsters in human shape, who boast of their liberty and of their humanity, while they carry the hearts of tigers within them. (Cheers.)—*Speech delivered at the Presentation of the Emancipation Society's Address to Mr. O'Connell,* 1835.

I hate slavery in all countries—the slavery of the Poles in Russia under their miscreant tyrant, and the slavery of the unfortunate men of color under their fellow-men, the boasted friends of liberty in the United States. Let the slave leap up for joy when he hears of the meeting of this day (cheers); let him have the prospect of freedom to cheer him in the decline of life. (Cheers.) We ought to make our exertions strongly, immediately, and unanimously. (Cheers.) Remember what is taking place elsewhere. Only cast your eye across the Atlantic, and see what is taking place on the American shores. (Cheers.) Behold those pretended sons of freedom—those who declared that every man was equal in the presence of his God —that every man had an inalienable right to liberty—behold them making, in the name of honor, their paltry honor, an organized resistance in Southern Slave States against the advocates of emancipation. Behold them aiding in the robbery committed on an independent State. See how they have seized upon the territory of Texas, taking it from Mexico, Mexico having totally abolished slavery without apprenticeship, (loud cheers,) in order to make it a new market for slavery. (Shame!) Remember how they have stolen, cheated, swindled, robbed that country, for the audacious and horrible purpose of perpetuating negro slavery. (Cries of "Shame!") Remember that there is now a treaty on foot, in contemplation at least, between the Texans and the President of the United States, and that it is only postponed till this robbery of Texas from Mexico can be completed. Oh! raise the voice of humanity against these horrible crimes! (Cheers.) There is about republicans a sentiment of pride—a feeling of self-exaltation. Let us tell these republicans, that instead of their being the highest in the scale of humanity, they are the basest of the base, the vilest of the vile. (Tremendous cheers.) My friends, there is a community of sentiment all over the world, borne on the wings of the press; and what the humble individual who is now addressing you may state, will be carried across the waves of the Atlantic; it will go up the Missouri—it will be wafted along the banks of the Mississippi—it will reach infernal Texas itself. (Immense cheering.) And though that pandemonium may scream at the sound, they shall suffer from the lash of human indignation applied to their horrible crime. (Cheers.) If they are not arrested in their career of guilt, four new States in America will be filled with slaves. Oh, hideous breeders of human beings for slavery! Such are the horrors of that system in the American States, that it is impossible, in this presence, to describe them; the mind is almost polluted by thinking of them. Should the measures now contemplated by the Americans be accomplished, these horrors will be increased fourfold; and men, with the human soul degraded, will be in a worse state even than the physical degradation of human bodies. (Cheers.) What have we to look to? Their honor—their generosity! We must expect nothing from their generosity. (Cheers.) Sir, I cannot restrain myself. It was only the other day, I read a letter in *The Morning Chronicle*, from their Philadelphia correspondent. A person, whose Indian name I forgot, (a voice, " Osecola,") but who was called Powell, had carried on a war at the head of the Seminoles, and other Florida tribes, against the people of Florida. He behaved nobly, and bravely fought for his country; and he would have been deified as a hero had he fought in a civilized nation, and testimonials would have been reared to commemorate his deeds, as great and numerous as those which have been raised to a Napoleon or a Wellington. But what happens to this warrior? Why, these Americans, having made a truce with him, invited him to a conference. He comes under the protection of that truce. Thus confiding in their honor, is he allowed to return? Oh no! He is not allowed to return, but is taken prisoner, and carried captive to the fort. (Shame, shame!) Oh, cry out shame, and let that cry be heard across the waves of the mighty ocean! (Cheers.) We are the teachers of humanity, we are the friends of humanity. What does it signify to us, that the crime is not committed on British soil! Wherever it is committed, we are its enemies. (Cheers.) The American, it is true, boasts of having been the first to abolish the slave trade carried on in foreign vessels. Why, he was. But what was the consequence? Every one of his own slaves at home was made of more value to him. It was a swindling humanity. It was worse than our twenty millions scheme. It had the guise of humanity, but had really the spirit of avarice and oppression. (Cheers.) I, perhaps, ought to apologize for detaining you (No, no! Go on!); but we are all children of the same Creator, heirs to the same promise, purchased by the blood of the same Redeemer, and what signifies of what caste, color or creed we may be? (Cheers.) It is our duty to proclaim that the cause of the negro is our cause, and that we will insist upon doing away, to the best of our human ability the

stain of slavery, not only from every portion of this mighty
empire, but from the face of the wlrole earth. (Cheers.) If
there be in the huts of Africa, or amidst the swamps of Texas,
a human being panting for liberty, let it be proclaimed to him
that he has friends and supporters among the great British
nation. (Cheers.)—*Speech delivered at a Public Meeting of
Anti-Slavery Delegates in London,* 1837.

It is utterly impossible that any thing should exist more
horrible than the American slave-breeding. The history of it
is this: The Americans abolished the foreign slave trade earlier
than England, but with this consolation—no small comfort to
so money-loving a race as the slaveholders—that by such
abolition, they enhanced the price of the slaves then in America,
by stopping the competition in the home market of newly im-
ported slaves. Why, otherwise, was not the home trade stopped
as well as the foreign? The reply is obvious.

To supply the home slave trade, an abominable, a most
hideous, most criminal, and most revolting practice of breeding negroes exclusively for sale, has sprung up, and especially,
we are told, in Virginia. There are breeding plantations for
producing negroes, as there are with us breeding farms for producing calves and lambs. And as our calf and lamb breeders
calculate the number of males of the flock to the females, similar calculations are made by the traffickers in human flesh.
One instance was mentioned to me of a human breeding farm
in America, which was supplied with two men and twelve
women. Why should I pollute my page with a description of
all that is immoral and infamous in such practice? But only
think of the wretched mothers, whom nature compels to love
their children—children torn from them for ever, just at the
period that they could requite their mother's love! The
wretched, wretched mother! Who can depict the mother's
distraction and madness? "But their maternal feelings are,"
says a modern writer, "treated with as much contemptuous
indifference, as those of the cows and ewes whose calves and
lambs are sent to the English market."

That it is which stains the character of the American slaveholder, and leaves the breeder of slaves the most detestable of
human beings; especially when that slaveholder is a republican, boasting of freedom, shouting for liberty, and declaring,
as the charter of his liberal institutions, these are self-evident
truths, "that all men are created equal—that they are endowed
by their Creator with certain inalienable rights—that among
these rights are life, liberty, and the pursuit of happiness."

My sole object in my speech at Birmingham, and present

object, is to rouse the attention of England and of Europe to all that is cruel, criminal, and, in every sense of the word, infamous, in the system of negro slavery in North America. My deliberate conviction is, that until that system is abolished, no American slaveholder ought to be received on a footing of equality by any of the civilized inhabitants of Europe.—*Letter of Mr. O'Connell to the Editor of the London Morning Chronicle*, 1838.

I have no superfluous tears to shed for Ireland, and shall show my love of my country by continuing my exertions to obtain for her justice and good government; but I feel that I have something Irish at my heart, which makes me sympathize with all those who are suffering under oppression, and forces me to give to universal man the benefit of the exertions which are the consequence. (Cheers.) And what adds peculiarly to the claim of Ireland for sympathy and support is, that in the great cause of suffering humanity, no voice was ever raised, but Ireland was found ready to afford relief and succor.—*Speech delivered at a Meeting of the British India Society, London*, 1839.

He then came to North America, and there, thank God, he found much reason for congratulation. There were now present forty representatives of American Abolition Societies to aid them in the great struggle for human liberty. Let them be honored, in proportion as the slave-holders were execrated. Oh! they had a hard battle to fight! In place of being honored as they were in this land, they had to encounter coolness and outrage; the bowie-knife and lynch law threatened them; they were Abolitionists at the risk of their lives. (Cheers.) Glory to them! A year or two since, he made some observations upon the conduct of the American Minister; he charged him with breeding slaves for sale; he denied it; and, in order to prove who was right, he sent him [Mr. O'Connell] a challenge to fight a duel. (Laughter.) He did not accept it. Nothing would ever induce him to commit murder. God had forbidden it, and he would obey him. (Cheers.) The American Minister denied the charge, but he admitted that he had slaves, and he admitted that he did afterwards sell some; so let him have the benefit of such a denial. (A laugh.) He added, however, that he did not believe that slaves were bred for sale in Virginia. Now, he would read some few extracts from Judge Jay's book, published in New York, in 1839. He would call Mr. Stevenson's attention to page 88 of that book, and that would prove to him, not only that slave-breeding existed in Virginia, but within twenty-five miles of his own residence [The Honorable Gentleman read several extracts, proving the practice; also several advertisements of lots of slaves wanted for ready money, for shipment to New Orleans, and dated in Richmond, the very place of Mr. Stevenson's residence.] He had established against the Ambassador, that slave-raising did exist in Virginia. Yet all these things took place in a civilized country—a civilized age—advertisements of human flesh for sale, and written 'in even a more contemptuous manner than if the subjects of them were cattle. The traffic in slaves from the North to the Southern States was immense. In the latter, they were put to the culture of sugar—a horrible culture, that swept off the whole in seven years—every seven years there was a new generation wanted. This was in a community calling themselves civilized. Why, they were worse than the savage beasts of the desert, for they only mangled when driven to it by hunger; but this horrible practice is carried on by well-fed Americans for paltry pecuniary profit—for that low and base consideration, they destroy annually their tens and twenty thousands.

These scenes took place in a country, which, in all other respects, had a fair claim to be called civilized—in a country which had nobly worked out its own freedom—in a country where the men were brave and the women beautiful. Amongst the descendants of Englishmen—even amongst such was to be found a horrible population, whose thirst for gold could only be gratified at the expense of such scenes of human suffering; a population who were insensible to the wrath of God, who were insensible to the cries and screams of mothers and children, torn from each other for ever. But there was one thing they would not be insensible to—they dare not, they would not be insensible to the contempt of Europe. (Loud cheers.) While they embraced the American Abolitionists as friends and brothers, let none of the slave-owners, dealers in human flesh, dare to set a foot upon our free soil. (Cheering.) Let them call upon the Government to protest to America, that they would not receive any slaveholding ambassador. (Loud cheering.) Let them declare that no slave-owner can be admitted into European society; and then Calhoun and Clay, and men like them, who stand up putting forth their claims to be President of the great Republic, must yield to the public, universal opinion. He had made mention of those two men—he would only say that Calhoun was branded with the blood issuing from the stripes of the slave, and Clay drowned in the tears of the mothers and the children. (Cheers.) Let the people of Europe say to slave-owners, " Murderers, you belong

2

not to us! Away to the desert, and herd with kindred savages!'' (Cheers.) He begged pardon of the savage. (Laughter.) Sometimes in anger he committed heinous crimes, but he was incapable of coolly calculating how long or how hard he could work a human being with a profit,—sometimes granting him a boon for the purpose of obtaining a year or two more of labor out of him. Well, are we to remain passive as hitherto? (Loud cries of "No, no!") Let our declaration also go abroad. Let this Society adopt it—let the benevolence and good sense of Englishmen make that declaration. If an American addresses you, find out at once if he be a slave-holder. (Hear, hear.) He may have business with you, and the less you do with him, the better (a laugh); but the moment that is over, turn from him as if he had the cholera or the plague (cheers)—for there is a moral cholera and a political plague upon him. (Cheers.) He belongs not to your country or your clime—he is not within the pale of civilization or Christianity. (Cheers.) Let us rally for the liberty of the human race (applause)—no matter in what country or in what clime he is found, the slave is entitled to our protection; no matter of what caste, of what creed, of what color, he is your fellow-man—he is suffering injustice; and British generosity, which has done so much already, ought to be cheered to the task by the recollection of the success it has already attained. (Cheers.) * * * I am zealous in the cause, to be sure, but inefficient—acknowledging the humility of the individual, I am still swelled by the greatness of the cause. My bosom expands, and I glory in the domestic struggle for freedom which gave me a title to stand among you, and to use that title in the best way I can, to proclaim humanity to man, and the abolition of slavery all over the world.—*Speech delivered at the Anniversary of the British and Foreign Anti-Slavery Society*, 1840.

From this spot, I wish to rouse all the high and lofty pride of the American mind. Republicanism necessarily gives a higher and prouder tone to the human mind than any other form of government. I am not comparing it with any thing else at present; but all history shows there is a pride about republicanism, which perhaps, is a consolation to the republican for any privations he may suffer, and a compensation for many things in which he may possibly be inferior; but from this spot, I repeat, I wish to rouse all the honesty and pride of American youth and manhood; and would that the voice of civilized Europe would aid me in the appeal, and swell my feeble voice to one shout of honest indignation ; and when these Americans point to their boasted Declaration of Independence, exclaim, "Look at your practice!" Can there be faith in man, or reliance placed in human beings, who thus contrast their action with their declarations? * * * That was the first phrase of their boasted Declaration of Independence. What was the last?—"To these principles we solemnly pledge our lives," (invoking the name of the great God, and calling for his aid,) "we solemnly pledge our lives, our fortunes, and our sacred honor." It has the solemnity without the profaneness of an oath; it speaks in the presence of the living God; it pledges life, fortune, and sacred honor to the principles they assert. How can they lay claim to "sacred honor," with this dark, emphatic, and diabolical violation of their principles staring them in the face? No! America must know that all Europe is looking at her, and that her Senate, in declaring that there is property in human beings, has violated her oath to God, and "sacred honor" to men. Will the American come down upon me, then, with his republicanism? I will meet him with the taunt, that he has mingled perjury with personal disgrace and dishonor, and inflicted both with a double barb into the character of any man who claims property in any human being. France, and even England, might possibly adopt such a resolution without violating their national honor, because they have made no such declarations as America, and therefore she is doubly dyed in disgrace by the course she has taken, in open opposition to her own charter of Independence. * * * I rejoice to hear the present agitation is striking terror into the hearts of the slave-mongers, whose selfish interests, vile passions, and predominant pride, with all that is bad and unworthy commingled, make them willing to retain their hold of human property, and to work with the bones and blood of their fellow-creatures; whilst a species of democratic aristocracy, the filthiest aristocracy that ever entered into civilized society, is set up in the several States—an aristocracy that wishes to have property without the trouble and toil of earning it, and to set themselves above men, only to plunder them of their natural rights, and to live solely upon their labor. Thus, the gratification of every bad passion, and every base emotion of the human mind is enlisted in defence of the slaveholder's right. When we turn our eyes upon America, we see in her Declaration of Independence the display of the democratic element of popular feeling against every thing like tyranny or oppression. But when I come to the District of Columbia, there I see in the capital and temple of freedom, the negro chained to his toil, and writhing beneath the lash of his taskmaster, and the negress doomed to all the horrors of slavery. There I see their infant, yet unable to understand what it is that tortures its father or distracts its mother; while that mother is cursing its existence, because it is not a man, but a slave; and almost wishing—ah! what a wringing thought to a mother's heart—that the child might sink into an early grave, rather than become the property of an excruciating tyrant, and the instrument of wealth to others, without being able to procure comfort and happiness for itself. That is America; that is the land of the free; these are the illustrations of the glorious principles laid down in the Declaration of American Independence! These evils, inflicted as they are by the democratic aristocracy of the States, are worse than ever were inflicted by the most kingly aristocracy, or the most despotic tyranny. I do not mean any thing offensive to our American friends present, but I do say, there is written in letters of blood upon the American escutcheon, robbery and murder, and plunder of human beings. I recognize no American as a fellow-man, except those who belong to anti-slavery societies. Those who uphold slavery are not men as we are, they are not honest as we are; and I look upon a slaveholder as upon a pickpocket, who violates the common laws of property and honesty.

They say that by their Constitution, they are prevented from emancipating the slaves in the slaveholding States; but I look in the Declaration of Independence, and the Constitution of 1787, and I defy them to find a single word about slavery, or any provision for holding property in man.

No man can deny the personal courage of the American people. With the recollections of the battles of Bunker's Hill and Saratoga,—of which, indeed, I might be reminded by the portrait which hangs opposite to me, of one of the officers who took an active part in those conflicts, (Earl of Moira,)—with the recollection, I say, of those battles it would be disgraceful and dishonest to deny to the American people personal courage and bravery. There exists not a braver people upon the face of the earth. But, amongst all those who composed the Convention of 1787, there was not one man who had the moral courage—I was about to say the immoral courage—to insert the word slavery in the Constitution. No! they did not dare pronounce the word; and if they did not dare to use the word slavery, are they to be allowed to adopt the thing? Is America to shake her star-spangled banner in the breeze, and boast of liberty, while she is conscious that that banner floats over the heads of slaves? Oh, but they call it "persons held to labor"—that is the phrase they use in their Constitution; but dare any one say that slavery is implied in those words? The term applies to any person who enters into a contract to labor, for a given period, as by the month or year, or for an equivalent; but his doing so does not constitute him a slave, surely; the very term is disgraceful to nature, and an affront to nature's God. No wonder the word was not in their declaration; you would not look to find words of injustice and cruelty in a declaration of honesty and humanity. I repeat it, they have not used the word. They meant slavery: they intended to have slaves, but they dared not employ the word; and " persons held to labor" was as near as they dared approach to it. Can you conceive of a deeper crime than slavery? A crime which includes in it injustice and cruelty, which multiplies robberies and murders! Ay, there is one thing worse even than this, and that is hypocrisy added to it. Let hypocrisy be superinduced on injustice, and you have, indeed, a character fit to mingle with the murky powers of darkness; and the Americans (I speak not of them all, there are many noble exceptions) have added hypocrisy to their other accomplishments. They say they have no power to emancipate their slaves: is that the real reason? It may be, that they have not power to do so in some particular States; but then, what shall be said of the District of Columbia? There they are not bound by any restriction; yet in that District there are slaves, and there they furnish further proof of their hypocrisy. Oh, say they, we are the finest gentlemen, the wisest statesmen, and most profound legislators in the world. We are ardent lovers of liberty, we detest slavery, and we lament that we have not the power to make all free. Then I whisper, Columbia! Columbia! You have the power there, you have the authority there, to remove this foul blot; you have the means and opportunities; you have, in short, every thing but the will: the will alone is wanting; and, with all your professions, you are hypocrites.

But I will now turn to a subject of congratulation: I mean the Anti-Slavery Societies of America—those noble-hearted men and women, who, through difficulties and dangers, have proved how hearty they are in the cause of abolition. I hail them all as my friends, and wish them to regard me as a brother. I wish for no higher station in the world; but I do covet the honor of being a brother with these American Abolitionists. In this country, the Abolitionists are in perfect safety; here we have fame and honor; we are lauded and encouraged by the good; we are smiled upon and cheered by the fair; we are bound together by godlike truth and charity; and though we have our differences as to points of faith, we have no differenee as to this point, and we proceed in our useful career esteemed and honored. But it is not so with our anti-slavery friends in America: there they are vilified, there they are insulted. Why, did not very lately a body of men—of gentlemen, so ealled—of persons who would be angry if you denied them that cognomen, and would even be ready to call you out to share a rifle and a ball—did not such "gentlemen" break in upon an Anti-Slavery Society in America; aye, upon a ladies' Anti-Slavery Society, and assault them in a most cowardly manner? And did they not denounee the members of that Soeiety? And where did this happen? Why, in Boston —in enlightened Boston, the capital of a non-slaveholding State. In this country, the Abolitionists have nothing to complain of; but in America, they are met with the bowie-knife and lynch law! Yes! in America, you have had martyrs; your cause has been stained with blood; the voice of your brethren's blood crieth from the ground, and riseth high, not, I trust, for vengeance, but for mercy, upon those who have thus treated them. But you ought not to be diseouraged, or relax in your efforts. Here you have honor. A human being cannot be placed in a more glorious position than to take up sueh a cause under such circumstances. I am delighted to be one of a Convention in which are so many of such great and good men. I trust that their reception will be such as that their zeal may be greatly strengthened to continue their noble struggle. I have reason to hope that, in this assembly, a voice will be raised which will roll back in thunder to America, which will mingle with her mighty waves, and which will cause one universal shout of liberty to be heard throughout the world. Oh, there is not a delegate from the Anti-Slavery Societies of America, but ought to have his name, aye, her name, written in characters of immortality! The Anti-Slavery Societies in America are deeply persecuted, and are deserving of every encouragement which we can possibly give them. I would that I had the eloquence to depiet their character aright; but my tongue falters, and my powers fail, while I attempt to describe them. They are the true friends of humanity, and would that I had a tongue to deseribe aright the mighty majesty of their undertaking! I love and honor America and the Americans. I respect their great principles; their untiring industry; their lofty genius; their social institutions; their morals, such morals as can exist with slavery—God knows they cannot be many— but I respect all in them or about them that is good. But, at the same time, I denounce and anathematize them as slave-holders, and hold them up to the scorn of all civilized Europe.

I would that the government of this country would tell the United States of America, that they must send no more slave-holding negotiators here!

I will tell you a little anecdote. Last year, I was accosted with great civility, by a well-dressed, gentleman-like person, in the lobby of the House of Commons. He stated that he was from America, and was anxious to be admitted to the House. "From what State do you come?" "From Alabama." "A slaveholder, perhaps?" "Yes." "Then," said I, "I beg to be excused;" and so I bowed and left him. Now, that is an example which I wish to be followed. Have no intercourse with a slaveholder. You may, perhaps, deal with him as a man of business, but, even then, you must act with caution, as you would with a pickpocket and a robber. You ought to be very scant of courtesy toward him, at least until he has cleared himself of the foul imputation. Let us beware of too much familiarity with such men; and let us plainly and honestly tell them, as a Convention, what we think of them. I am not for the employment of force; no—let all be done by the statement of indisputable facts; by the diffusion of information; by the union of benevolent minds; by our bold determination to expose tyranny and cruelty; by proclaiming to the slaveholders that, so long as they have any connection with the accursed traffic in human beings, we hold them to be a different race. Why should it not be so? Why should we not shrink from them, as we would with shuddering from the approach of the vilest reptiles? The declaration of such views and feelings from such a body of men as are now before me, will make the slaveholders tremble. My voice is feeble, but I have no doubt but what I say will reach them, and that it will have some influence upon them. They must feel that they cannot much longer hold the sway. One of the great objects of my hope is to affright the Americans by laying hold upon their pride, their vanity, their self-esteem, by commending what is excellent in them, and by showing how very far they come short in those proprieties upon which they boast themselves. I would have this Convention avail themselves of all such aids, and to urge them by every possible argument to abandon the horrid vice by which their character is so foully disfigured. * * * We have proof this day that there are those who love the cause of freedom in every part of the globe. And why should it not be so? Why should not all unite in such a glorious cause? We are all formed by the same Creator; we are alike the objects of the same watchful Providence; we are all the purchase of the same redeeming blood; we have one

common Saviour; and our hearts beat high with the same immortal hopes. And why should any portion of the human
race be shut out from our affection and regard? * * * O, let
our word go forth from this place, that we do not deem the
Americans Christians, by whatever name they are called,
whether Episcopalians, er·Baptists, or Independents, or Metho-
dists, or whatever other name,—that we regard them not as
Christians at all, unless they cordially unite with us in this
great work. We honor all that is really good in America, and
would have it all on our side in this glorious struggle—in this
holy cause. Let us unite and persevere, and, by the blessing
of God, and the aid of good men, freedom will, ere long, wave
her triumphant banner over emancipated America, and we
shall unite with the whole world to rejoice in the result.—
*Speech at the World's Anti-Slavery Convention, held in Free-
mason's Hall, London, June,* 1840.

At a Special meeting of the Loyal National Repeal Association, held in the Great Room, Corn Exchange, Dublin, May,
9, 1843,—JAMES HAUGHTON, Esq., in the chair,—

Mr. O'Connell said :—The Association had adjourned to
that day for the purpose of receiving a communication with
which they had been honored from the Anti-Slavery Society
of America—a body of men whom they most entirely respect
—whose objects should be cherished in their hearts' core—
whose dangers enhanced their virtues—and whose persevering
patriotism would either write their names on the pages of tem-
poral history, or impress them in a higher place, where eternal
glory and happiness would be the reward of their exertions.
(Cheers.) His impressions were so strong in favor of the Anti-
Slavery Society of America, that he thought it would not be
so respectful as he would desire, if he brought forward that
document in the routine of business on the last day, when it
could not be so much attended to as it deserved. (Hear, hear.)
It was out of respect to the people who sent that document, that
they had adjourned ; and he might say, that personal respect
for the Chairman was mixed up with that consideration. (Cheers.)
They could not have sent a better message, or a more sincere
one ; and, if he now had the kindness to make the communication, they would receive it with the respect it deserved.
(Cheers.)

The Anti-Slavery Address having been read,—

Mr. O'Connell then said :—I rise with the greatest alacrity
to move that that most interesting document be inserted on the
minutes, and that the fervent thanks of the Repeal Association
of Ireland be by acclamation voted to the writers of it. I

never in my life heard anything read that imposed more upon my feelings, and excited a deeper sympathy and sorrow within me. I never, in fact, before knew the horrors of slavery in their genuine colors. It is a production framed in the purest effort of simplicity, but, at the same time, powerful in its sentiments, so at once to reach the human heart, and stir up the human feelings to sorrow and execration—sorrow for the victims, and execration for the tyrants. (Loud cries of hear, hear, and cheers.) It will have its effect throughout Ireland; for the Irish people did not know what was, alas! familiar to you, Sir, and to me,—the real state of slavery in America, and of the unequaled evils it inflicts; for slavery, wherever it exists, is the bitterest potion that can be commended to the lips of man. Let it be presented in any shape, and it must disgust, for a curse inherent to it grows with it, and inflicts oppression and cruelty wherever it descends. (Hear, hear, and cheers.) We proclaim it an evil; and though, as a member of this Association, I am not bound to take up any national quarrel, still, I do not hesitate to declare my opinions; I never paltered in my own sentiments. (Cheers.) I never said a word in mitigation of slavery in my life; and I would consider myself the most criminal of human beings if I had done so. (Hear, and cheers.)

Yes, I will say, shame upon every man in America, who is not an anti-slavery man; shame and disgrace upon him! I don't care for the consequences. I will not restrain my honest indignation of feeling. I pronounce every man a faithless miscreant, who does not take a part for the abolition of slavery. (Tremendous cheering for several minutes.) It may be said that offence will be taken at these words. Come what may from them, they are my words. (Renewed applause.) The question never came regularly before us until now. We had it introduced collaterally; we had it mentioned by persons who were friends of ours, and who were endeavoring to maintain good relations between us and the slaveholders, but it is only now that it comes directly before us. We might have shrunk from the question by referring the document to a committee; but, I would consider such a course unworthy of me, enjoying as I do the confidence of the virtuous, the religious, and the humane people of Ireland; for I would be unfit to be what I desire to consider myself, the representative of the virtues of the people, if I were not ready to make every sacrifice for them, rather than to give the least sanction to human slavery.

They say that the slaves are worse treated since the cry of the

Abolitionists has been raised in their favor, as it has made their masters more suspicious of them, and more severe against them; but has that any weight with me? How often was I told, during our agitation, that "the Catholics would be emancipated but for the violence of that O'Connell!" (Laughter.) Why, one of the cleverest men in the country wrote a pamphlet in 1827, in which he stated that the Protestants of Ireland would have emancipated their Catholic countrymen long before, but for me, and fellows of my kind; and yet, two years after, I got emancipation in spite of them. (Cheers.) But it is clearly an insult to the understanding to speak so. When did tyranny relax its gripe merely because it ought to do so? (Hear.) As long as their was no agitation, the masters enjoyed the persecution of their slaves in quietness; but the moment the agitation commenced, they cried out, "Oh, it is not the slaves we are flogging, but we are flogging through his back the anti-slavery men." (Laughter.) But the subject is too serious for ridicule. I am afraid they will never give up slavery until some horrible calamity befalls their country; and I here warn them against the event, for it is utterly impossible that slavery can continue much longer. (Hear, hear.) But, good Heaven! can Irishmen be found to justify, or rather to palliate, (for no one could dare attempt to justify,) a system which shuts out the book of human knowledge, and seeks to reduce to the condition of a slave, 2,500,000 human beings: which closes against them not only the light of human science, but the rays of divine revelation, and the doctrines which the Son of God came upon the earth to plant! The man who will do so belongs not to my kind. (Hear, hear.) Over the broad Atlantic I pour forth my voice, saying, "Come out of such a land, you Irishmen; or, if you remain, and dare countenance the system of slavery that is supported there, we will recognize you as Irishmen no longer." (Hear, hear, and cheers.)

I say the man is not a Christian,—he cannot believe in the binding law of the Decalogue. He may go to the chapel or the church, and he may turn up the whites of his eyes, but he cannot kneel as a Christian before his Creator, or he would not dare to palliate such an infamous system. No, America! the black spot of slavery rests upon your star-spangled banner; and no matter what glory you may acquire beneath it, the hideous, damning stain of slavery rests upon you, and a just Providence will sooner or later avenge itself for your crime. (Loud and continued cheers.) Sir, I have spoken the sentiments of the Repeal Association. (Renewed cheers.) There is not a man amongst the hundreds of thousands that belong to our body, or amongst the millions that will belong to it, who does not concur in what I have stated. We may not get money from America after this declaration; but even if we should not, we do not want blood-stained money. (Hear, hear.) If they make it the condition of our sympathy, or if there be implied any submission to the doctrine of slavery on our part, in receiving their remittance, let them cease sending it at once. But there are wise and good men every where, and there are wise and good men in America—and that document which you have read, Sir, is a proof, among others, that there are ; and I would wish to cultivate the friendship of such men; but the criminals and the abettors—those who commit, and those who countenance the crime of slavery—I regard as the enemies of Ireland, and I desire to have no sympathy or support from them. (Cheers.)

I have the honor to move that this document be inserted in full upon our minutes, and that the most grateful thanks of the Repeal Association be given to the Anti-Slavery Society of America, who sent it to us, and in particular, to the two office bearers, whose names are signed to it.

At a meeting of the Loyal National Repeal Association, in Dublin, August 8, 1843, Mr. O'Connell, in the course of a powerful Anti-Slavery speech, said :—

A disposition was evinced in America to conciliate the opinion of that Association in favor of the horrid system of slavery, but they refused, of course, to show any sanction to it. (Hear, and cheers.)

He had taken an active part in the Anti-Slavery Society from the moment that he was competent to discover any one body of men acting for the extinction of slavery all over the world ; and he stood in that Association as the representative of the Irish people, who had themselves suffered centuries of persecution, because they were attached to humanity, and to what justice and reason demanded ; for if they had chosen to be silent, and had bowed to authority—if they had acquiesced in the dictation of their masters and tyrants, they would have escaped many temporary sufferings, but they would not have acquired the glory of having adhered with religious fidelity to their principles. Standing as their representative, he could not act otherwise than he had done, though the liberty of Ireland, the repeal of the Union itself, were to abide the result. He was bound not to look to consequences, but to justice and humanity; and come what would, he did not hesitate to throw heart and soul into his opposition to the system that would treat human beings as brute beasts of the field. He spoke distinctly and emphatically, for as he wanted to make an impression, he used harder words than he would have done, if he did not know that harsh words were necessary to rouse the selfish temperament of the domineering master of slaves. And he did make that sensation, and he was glad of it.

At a meeting of the Loyal National Repeal Association, held in Conciliation Hall, Dublin, Sept. 29th, 1845, Mr. O'Connell, speaking on the subject of American slavery, said:

I have been assailed for attacking the American institution, as it is called, negro slavery. I am not ashamed of that attack—I do not shrink from it. I am the advocate of civil and religious liberty all over the globe, and wherever tyranny exists, I am the foe of the tyrant; wherever oppression shows itself, I am the foe of the oppressor; wherever slavery rears its head, I am the enemy of the system, or the institution, call it by what name you will. (Great cheering.) I am the friend of liberty in every clime, class, and color:—my sympathy with distress is not confined within the narrow bounds of my own green island—no, it extends itself to every corner of the earth—my heart walks abroad, and wherever the miserable is to be succored, and the slave is to be set free, there my spirit is at home, and I delight to dwell in its abode. (Enthusiastic cheering.) It has been asked, What business has O'Connell to interfere with American slavery? Why, do not the Americans show us their sympathy for our struggles, and why should we not show a sympathy in efforts for liberty amongst themselves? (Cheers.) But I confess I have another strong reason for desiring to abolish slavery in America. In no monarchy on the face of the earth is there such a thing as domestic slavery. It is true, in some colonies belonging to monarchies, slavery exists; but in no European country is there slavery at all, for the Russian serf is far different from the slave of America, and therefore I do not wish that any lover of liberty should be able to draw a contrast between the democratic republic of America and the despotic States of Europe. (Hear, hear.) I am in favor of the democratic spirit, and I wish to relieve it from the horrors of slavery. (Cheers.) I do not wish to visit America with force and violence—I would be the last man in the world to consent to it. I would not be for making war to free the negro; at least not for the war of knife, and lash, and sword; but I would be for the moral warfare—I would be for the arms of argument and humanity to procure the extinction of tyranny, and to hurl contempt and indignation on those who call themselves freemen, and yet keep others in slavery. I would bring elements of that kind to bear upon the system, until the very name of slavery should be regarded with horror in the republic of America. (Cheers.) *   ·*   *   *

In the year '25, when I left my profession and went over to England, there was an anti-slavery meeting, at which I was present and spoke; and afterward, when I went to Parliament, another meeting was appointed, greater in magnitude. The West India interest was 27 strong in the House of Commons—the Algerine bill was carried through the House by a majority of 19—therefore, the emancipation bill was in the power of the West India interest; but when they sent a respected friend of mine (the Knight of Kerry) to me, to ask why I did not take a certain course with regard to it, what was my answer? "I represent the Irish people here, and I will act as the Irish people will sanction. Come liberty, come slavery to myself, I will never countenance slavery, at home or abroad!" (Cheers.) I said I came here on principle; the Irish people sent me here to carry out their principles; their principles are abhorrent of slavery; and, therefore, I will take my part at that anti-slavery meeting; and though it should be a blow against Ireland, it is a blow in favor of human liberty, and I will strike that blow. (Cheers.) So far was I from cultivating the slavery interest, that I adopted that course, though I regretted to lose their votes. But I must do them the credit to say, that I did not lose them. They acted nobly, and said they would not revenge upon Ireland my attack upon them. (Cheers.) * * Let them blame me—in America let me be execrated by them—let their support be taken from Ireland—Slavery, I denounce you wherever you are! (Loud cheers.) Come freedom, come oppression to Ireland—let Ireland be as she may—I will have my conscience clear before my God. (Continued cheers.) * * *

They were told that the speech he made in that room would put an end to the remittances from America; and that the Americans would not again contribute to the funds of the Association. If they should never get one shilling from America, his course was plain, his path was obvious. He was attached to liberty; he was the uncompromising hater of slavery wherever it was to be found. (Cheers.)

Have I traduced the Americans, when I talked of the horrors of domestic slavery? I happened to receive a New Orleans paper, published in the centre of domestic slavery—it is called the *Jeffersonian Republic*, and I shall read an extract from it. By that I perceive that, in connection with the institution of slavery in New Orleans—for I find that, in America, they call it an institution—there are public whipping places; men are licensed to keep shambles of torture (hear, hear); the master sends his slave to those shambles, there to get one hundred lashes, and the man gets the hundred lashes, or whatever degree of punishment his master desires. (Hear, hear.) There are actually shambles kept there for the torture of slaves, and there are persons who earn a livelihood—what a hideous livelihood!—by flogging human beings at the instance of those who are called their masters. (Hear, hear.) Am I to blame if I attack a system of that kind? (Hear, hear.) Male or female, young or old, whipped at the discretion of a man whose only limit is not actually killing the individual! (Hear, hear.) They would thus make the slave declare whether he is guilty of a theft or not. Are they, I ask, Christian men who endure to see these scenes going on around them? (Hear, hear.) Recollect that this is not the statement of a calumniator, or a libeler, or foreign emissary, but it is the statement published in the darkest hole of slavery, New Orleans itself. (Hear, hear.)—*Speech before the Dublin Repeal Association, September*, 1844.

ADDRESS

FROM THE MEMBERS OF THE CUFFE-LANE TEMPERANCE SOCIETY TO THEIR BRETHREN IN AMERICA.

DUBLIN, February, 1847.

To IRISHMEN IN AMERICA;

COUNTRYMEN: From recent information that we have received on the subject of slavery, as it exists in the country of your adoption, our hearts have been warmed afresh with zeal on behalf of freedom, and our sympathies re-kindled in favor of the American slave, who is deprived of all his rights, and subjected to the irresponsible will of his master.

Countrymen! our hearts burn with indignation at the thoughts of this injustice to our fellow-creatures, who are children of the same God as we are, and destined to a similar glorious end.

We have heard, fellow-countrymen, with feelings of deep sorrow, that many of you are indifferent to the wrongs of the slave, and that some are to be found even in the ranks of those who chain, and whip, and lacerate him; and who, without pity or remorse, forcibly separate husbands and wives, parents and children, selling them at the auction-table to the highest bidder!

By all your memories of Irishmen, by all your love of Fatherland, we entreat you not to disgrace the land of your birth, by aiding the tyrant in the land of your adoption to rivet the chains on his victim!

What right have you to enslave the colored man? Did not God create him in His own image as well as you? If you are authorized to keep him in bondage, show us your license from the Lord of earth and heaven!

God has placed an instinct within your bosoms, which tells you that "man is created free and equal, and that all are alike entitled to life, liberty, and the pursuit of happiness."

Countrymen! we appeal to you in the name of the Declaration of Independence, which guarantees to every inhabitant of the United States of America the priceless boon of liberty, but which instrument has been basely trampled under foot, in relation to three millions of the people of that republic.

On the fourth day of July, every year, you and every citizen of America celebrate your freedom from political servitude. Perform this act of hypocrisy no more, until the colored man can unite in the joyful hymn of thanksgiving.

In a word, countrymen, we call upon you to be true to the principles of Liberty and Justice. Pursue a contrary course, and you will disgrace your country, and impede her advancement on the road of freedom.

We need your sympathy, as you need ours, for the promotion of the principles of Truth and Justice at home and abroad; and neither of us can help the other, if we are false to God's light in our own hearts.

We remain, countrymen and friends, faithfully yours,

JOHN SPRATT, D. D., *President of the Society*,
Chapel House, Angier St., Dublin.

JAMES HAUGHTON—*and 881 others.*

TRIBUTE TO THE MEMORY OF O'CONNELL.

[From the Annual Report of the Massachusetts A. S. Society, 1847.]

The last year has been marked in the annals of Ireland, and of the world, by the death of the great O'Connell. This is no place to recount his history or to pronounce his eulogy.

It is for others to tell his labors in behalf of the great movements for the Relief of his Religion, for the Reform of Parliament, and for the Repeal of the Union. But to his earnestness in the cause of West Indian Emancipation, his readiness to denounce the Colonization imposture when exposed to him by Mr. Garrison, his indignant contempt of slaveholders and their apologists, and his consistent hatred of Slavery and readiness to co-operate with the Abolitionists, we may be permitted to pay the tribute of our admiration and gratitude. He died at Genoa, on the 15th of May, 1847, in the 72d year of his age, while upon a pilgrimage to the metropolis of his ancient Faith, of which he was ever a zealous votary and a duteous son. But his frame was too much shattered by his toils and sufferings to permit him to reach the Head of his Church. Few men have left behind them a more famous name, or one that excites more opposite emotions in the hearers' minds. No one of his times was better hated and better loved than he. No man's character was submitted to such opposite constructions. But when the evil and the good that he has left behind him shall be pondered in the impartial balance of posterity, we believe that his services in the cause of civil and religious liberty, his recognition of moral power and the renunciation of violence and bloodshed of his later years, will be found to outweigh his errors, and that he will be recognized as among the foremost of the friends of mankind.

www.ingramcontent.com/pod-product-compliance
Lightning Source LLC
Chambersburg PA
CBHW061239260626
47172CB00003B/934